Reinhart Brandau

Three Birds of Prey
from
Three Bird-Moons

Drei Greifvögel
aus
Drei Vogelmonde

English and German
Englisch und Deutsch
Reinhart Brandau

Fotos
Reinhart Brandau, Nadine Gerloff, Karl Gieseke

copyright 2012 Reinhart Brandau

Herstellung und Verlag:
BoD – Books on Demand, Norderstedt
ISBN 978-3-7322-3405-9

Born 1936 in the Thuringian Forest, Reinhart Brandau´s adventurous life came to a highlight when he made friends with Mecki the hooded crow in spring 1987. He worked at "Weser-Flugzeugbau" till 1962 and took part at the constructing of the first Airbus C 160. Afterwards he started his career of an artist as silversmith, sculptor and painter up to the day, when his friends the wild birds, and the documenting of their adventurous bird life, took him up completely.

1936 im Thüringer Wald geboren, erreichte Reinhart Brandau´s abenteuerliches Leben mit dem Erscheinen der Nebelkrähe Mecki, im Frühjahr 1987, seinen vorläufigen Höhepunkt. Er arbeitete im „Weser-Flugzeugbau" bis 1962, und war an der Konstruktion des ersten Airbus C 160 beteiligt. Danach begab er sich auf seine künstlerische Laufbahn als Silberschmied, Bildhauer und Maler, bis ihn seine Freunde die Wildvögel, und die Dokumentation ihres abenteuerlichen Vogellebens, ganz in Besitz nahmen.

I now want to say thank you to my friends Nadine Gerloff and Karl Gieseke for helping me to create this book, for a lot of photos, and for the essential support to heal the buzzard's broken leg. Thanks also to my friend Rolf W. Schwake, who helped me with words and deeds at the final work on this manuscript.

Dank sagen möchte ich meinen Freunden Nadine Gerloff und Karl Gieseke für die Unterstützung und Hilfe bei der Erstellung dieses Buches, für die vielen Photos und auch für die einfühlsame Behandlung, mit der Nadine das gebrochene Bein des Bussards gerettet hat. Auch bei meinem Freund Rolf W. Schwake möchte ich mich bedanken, der mir bei der endgültigen Manuskriptüberarbeitung mit Rat und Tat zur Seite stand.

Winter

December 17th in Worpswede ...

plenty of snow still covers this winter-land – bitter cold – great distress and they will turn
up: birds, squirrels, here, by my door ... and they are my friends, all of them – especially the
little great-tit-girl of course: that tousled one, she really suits me ...

17. Dezember in Worpswede ...

noch liegt viel Schnee auf dem Winterland – bitterkalt – groß die Not und finden sich ein:
Vögel wie Eichhörnchen, bei mir, vor meiner Tür ... und sind alles meine Freunde –
besonders die kleine Meisenfrau: verstrubbelt wie sie ist, paßt sie doch so gut zu mir ...

current photo of my lap …   aktuelles Photo meines Schoßes …

dining peacefully with each other ...   friedlich speisen sie miteinander ...

disputing a little, very human ...   kleine Streitigkeiten, sehr menschlich ...

may be they are dancing together, who knows ... oder tanzen sie miteinander?, wer weiß ...

more and more come flying in ...   immer mehr kommen angeflogen ...

peacefull all together …   und vertragen sich alle …

all of them my friends ...   alles meine Freunde ...

if I should ever get hold of an enemy of my friends, what would I do then? ...

sollte mir aber jemals ein Feind meiner Freunde in die Hände fallen,

was würde ich mit dem wohl machen? ...

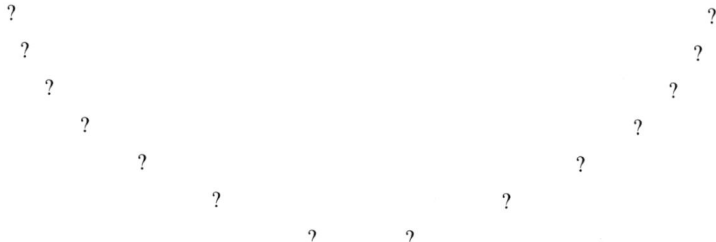

December 19th 9.20 a.m.

a great big hunter appears at the door, presenting a buzzard in his huge gloved hand – looks
at me miserably, the bird – found him lying in the snow, says the hunter-man …

19. Dezember 9.20 Uhr

in der Haustür erscheint ein großer Jäger, hält einen Bussard in seiner riesigen rechten
Handschuhhand – schaut mich an wie das heulende Elend, der Vogel – lag im Schnee, sagt
der Jägersmann …

my bare hands loosen the poor creature out of that glove-grip, feeling just bones underneath
feathers, and a throbbing heart …
can´t stand any more, already too weak – don´t want him to lay down either, the proud bird –
carefully I stand him on a wooden bar of the paint-easel and lean him against a prop so he will
not fall over … standing on his right claw while the left one is dangling down before him,
motionless, looks like he´s creeping inside himself …

meine bloßen Hände lösen das Elend aus dem Handschuhgriff, fühlen nur Knochen unter
Federn, und ein puckerndes Herz …
kann nicht mehr stehen, schon zu schwach – liegen soll er aber auch nicht, der stolze Vogel –
stell ihn vorsichtig auf ein Querholz der Staffelei, an ein Holz gelehnt, daß er nicht umfällt …
auf die halb geschlossene rechte Hand gestellt, die linke hängt vor ihm herab, hängt er reglos
in den Seilen –

thinks, may be, he´s already gone to the other world, world of no return …

wähnt sich wahrscheinlich schon im Jenseits, wo nichts irdisches mehr geht …

in a great hurry; I cut up raw salmon into small pieces, warm water-bath, electrolyte-dip,
I also sprinkle a little glucose on it and some drops of multivitamin and … probably he´s ima-
gining that he´s flying about with the angels by now and doesn't feel like ever wanting to
open his beak again –

nun aber schnell! meinen rohen Lachs zerteilen, Warmwasserbad, in kleine Häppchen schnei-
den, in Elektrolytwasser tunken, kleine Messerspitze Traubenzucker drüber streuen, paar
Tropfen Multivitamin und … der fliegt ja in Gedanken schon mit den Engeln rum und denkt
nicht dran, seinen Schnabel nochmal aufzumachen –

while left forefinger and thumb hold the beak, right fingers slightly drag the lower part of the
beak downwards – slowly the throat opens … left fingers in from the side to keep it open
while I put a small piece of salmon in … the bird is puzzled, doesn´t understand what this is
all about – I do understand: he must swallow the bite – so I slip it with my forefinger into the
throat and stroke it downward till poor boy, I reckon, swallows it at last …

linker Zeigefinger und Daumen halten den Schnabel – rechte Finger ziehen Federn an unterer
Schnabelhälfte leicht nach unten – langsam öffnet sich der Rachen … linke Finger seitlich
rein, damit er offen bleibt, und ein kleines Häppchen Lachs hinein … der Vogel wundert sich
nur, und weiß nicht – ich schon: er soll das Häppchen schlucken – schiebe es mit dem Zeigefinger weit in seinen Schlund hinein und streichele es hinab - bis der Junge, denk ich mal, es
endlich runterschluckt …

having swallowed the third force-fed bite, he slowly returns into a somewhat completely
different, unknown kind of being and takes the remaining bites, as though it couldn't be
otherwise, gently off my fingers …

nach dem dritten „Zwangshappen" kehrt er sachte in´s für ihn ganz neue Hier zurück, und
nimmt die restlichen Happen Lachs nun ganz zwanglos, wie selbstverständlich, vorsichtig von
meinen Fingern …

9.45 a.m.
having been able to describe the outer interactions of my guest and me precisely, I wouldn't
dare though; even try to narrate the interactions occuring between this wild bird and me,
under feathers, skin and hair …

9.45
so präzise ich das äußere Geschehen zwischen meinem Gast und mir schildern konnte, so
wenig könnte ich über das berichten, was in dieser Zeit zwischen dem Wildvogel und mir,
unter Federn, Haut und Haaren noch geschehen ist …

$12^{\circ\circ}$ a.m.
it seems that these few morsels of salmon have been just the right food for my guest – in the
meantime he has recovered so far, that he went off his place on the paint-easel, and got onto a
box where he apparently prefers to be – now he gets easily digestable beef-meat, which
heconsiders to be a very tasty treat …

das bißchen Lachs muß für meinen Gast genau das richtige gewesen sein – er hat sich inzwischen soweit erholt, daß er seinen Platz auf der Staffelei verlassen hat und auf eine Kiste gelangt ist, auf der er sich wohlzufühlen scheint – nun bekommt er erstmal noch leicht verdauliches Rindergulasch, das er mit großem Appetit Verzehrt …

my big friend gets few small bites only, per hour – nearly having starved to death, too much food all of a sudden might kill him, after all …

ich gebe ihm aber nur kleine Portionen, alle Stunde ein wenig – ausgehungert wie er ist, könnte es ihn umbringen, wenn er alles auf einmal bekäme …

December 20th

early this morning, my new friend awaits me on the big table – bearing a warmed up black frozen mouse in my right hand and a camera in the left, I go towards him – disgusted, his shoulders slightly rased in defence, the big bird retreats; this mouse shall I eat? – what a thing to ask for! – alas! it is quite black! … something similar, my bird may be thinking about all this, it certainly has never seen a black mouse before – they don't appear in nature, I think …

20. Dez.

am frühen Morgen erwartet mich mein neuer Freund auf dem großen Tisch – eine aufgetaute
Tiefkühlmaus in der rechten Hand, meine Kamera in der linken, geh ich zu ihm – empört, die
Flügel in Abwehr leicht gehoben, weicht er vor der Maus zurück; was? die soll ich essen?
die ist ja ganz schwarz! ... so, oder so ähnlich, denkt mein Vogel wohl, hat gewiß noch nie
eine schwarze Maus gesehen – kommt ja in freier Wildbahn auch nicht vor ...

in spite of his displeasure about the mouse, I keep offering it to my bird-guest encouraging
him to taste it at least, and – indeed, he takes the mouse after all – like tiptoeing, holding it
merely with the tip of his beak, not wanting to have it get too close and – drops it on the
spot, looks at that black thing closely from every side, turns it over with his hooked beak,
nibbles a little at the head of the mouse and – begins to eat the little creature at last ...

biete sie ihm dennoch weiter an und ermutige ihn, sie doch wenigstens mal zu probieren, und
– tatsächlich nimmt er sie nun doch – mit der Schnabelspitze nur, daß sie ihm bloß nicht zu
nah kommt und – läßt sie gleich wieder fallen, betrachtet das schwarze Etwas eingehend von
allen Seiten, dreht es mit seinem Hakenschnabel um, knabbert ein wenig am Mausekopf her
um und – fängt endlich an, das kleine Tier zu verspeisen ...

I now provide as much food for the big bird as he chooses to devour – he spreads his protecting wings over his "prey" - so there will not be any dispute about who it belongs to …

nun gebe ich dem großen Vogel so viel zu essen wie er verschlingen mag – dabei breitet er die Flügel schützend über seine „Beute", daß sie ihm niemand streitig macht …

fortunately the other one isn´t alive …   nur gut, daß der andere nicht lebendig ist …

reproachful glare – meat-bowl is empty! …   vorwurfsvoller Blick – Fleischschale leer ! …

don´t you have any more for me? …   hast du denn gar nichts mehr für mich? …

no? I don´t believe you! …   nein? glaub ich dir nicht! …

didn´t I know it?! …   hab´s doch gewußt! …

flying more speedily than the poor camera is able to think – tut mir leid …

fliegt wieder schneller als die arme Kamera denken kann – sorry …

I want to get out of here ...   will raus aus dieser engen Bude ...

out over there where there is plenty of space to fly ... hangin on the gauze which,
cushioning, will avoid a crash ...

nach da draußen, wo mehr Platz zum fliegen ist ... hängt an der Gaze, die, abfedernd, einen
Aufprall verhindert ...

really must get higher, by all means! ...   auch will ich höher, unbedingt! ...

days are floating past, like colourful fishes in the ocean of time on their way back to the
worldsoulocean – sanctuary of eternity …

Tage schwimmen vorüber, wie bunte Fische im Meer der Zeit, auf ihrem Weg zurück ins
Weltenseelenmeer – dem Hort der Ewigkeit …

Buzzi, deep in thought, just like me … Bussi, in Gedanken versunken, so, wie ich auch …
the day of freedom, when will it be? …
wann kommt der Tag an dem ich endlich wieder fliegen kann, wohin ich will? …

December 31th 12°°
thirteen days, my big friend and I have accompanied each other in life – while I fed him
meaty food, this remarkable bird influence by its closeness, its calm solemn life force, and
beauty, enabled me to assemble my thoughts and emotions and put them in such a way
into words, that they might touch you, reading these lines …

31. Dezember 2011 12°°
dreizehn Tage haben wir, mein großer Freund und ich, einander durch´s Leben begleitet –
während ich ihn mit fleischlicher Kost versorgte half er mir, mit seiner Nähe, seiner ruhigen
Lebenskraft und Schönheit, meine Gedanken und Gefühle so zu vereinen, und in Worte zu
kleiden, daß sie dich vielleicht berühren, wenn du diese Zeilen liest …

still very cold, and plenty of snow – and I ask myself whether I can take responsibility for
allowing my guest to fly to his freedom, in spite of it … I´d rather he´d stay some more days –
but, locked in, here in the bird room, while outside the fireworks-hell bursts out?! …
it´s like having a choice between plague and cholera, and I must decide … and I think, it´s
better for him to be out in nature then, although there will be plenty broken wings and necks
… at this night of terror …

Kälte und Schnee noch immer – kann ich es verantworten meinen Gast trotzdem schon in seine ersehnte Freiheit fliegen zu lassen? … würde ihn ja gerne noch ein paar Tage bei mir haben – aber eingesperrt im Vogelzimmer, wenn draußen die Feuerwerkshölle losbricht? – da ist er draußen wohl besser aufgehoben auch wenn es dort so manchen Hals- und Flügel-bruch geben wird … in dieser Terrornacht …

the civilized mankind herd isn't aware anymore of what it is doing – brainwashed, it will follow any bell-wether anywhere, will be led astray by any stupid advertising to any kind of nonsense … the manner in which it celebrates New Year's Eve, in this country anyway, is painful evidence … civilized mankind herd greeting the New Year with fire and bangs as punctual as clockwork – herd-members have compared watches – not one hundredth of a second shall be missed by sleeping, as though life depends on it … nine, eight, seven, six, five, four, THREE, TWO, ONE, HURRRRAAAAAH!!! CHEEERS!
HAPPY NEW YEAR!!!

die zivilisierte Menschenherde weiß ja nicht mehr was sie tut – fremdbestimmt folgt sie jedem Leithammel überallhin, läßt sich von der primitivsten Werbung zu jedem Unsinn verführen – die Neujahrsfeier hierzulande ist dafür der schönste, zugleich recht peinliche Beweis … das Neue Jahr begrüßen, mit Feuer und Krach, auf die Sekunde pünktlich – Uhrenvergleich, nachstellen wo nötig – nicht eine hundertstel Sekunde darf verschlafen werden – als gelte es das Leben … neun, acht, sieben, sechs, fünf, vier, DREI, ZWEI, EINZ, HURRAAAAA!!!!
PROST NEUJAAAAHR!!!! EIN GUTES JAHR 20XX!!! …

all good wishes in vain – with this stupid mankind herd, a good year?! – rather will cows learn to fly – alas! and what is more: in spite of having compared watches … it, all the herd, has slept away missing the new year by eightysix million fourhundredthousand hundredths of a second, accounts to: eighthundredsixtifourthousand seconds, twohundredfourty hours or ten days … actually, the new year begins on 22th of December at winter solstice when the second of the two longest nights of the year, begins, and the days last longer as the sun rises higher up every day – then the new year has begun … but, alas! the devil lurks anywhere – that´s why, once upon a time, a certain Silvestre wet himself on December the twentyfirst and, because of that, he would n´t greet the new year before December the thirtyfirst, when he was dry again – so he hailed this New Year which has, in the meantime, grown ten days old, and, being one of these bell-wethers, he commanded the first of January to be both: Silvestre and the first day of the new year …

alle guten Wünsche vergeblich – mit dieser geistlosen Menschenherde ein gutes Jahr?! ehr
lernt eine Kuh fliegen – und außerdem, trotz Uhrenvergleich … hat sie, die ganze Herde, das
Neue Jahr doch tatsächlich verschlafen … um nicht weniger als 10 x X hundertstel Sekunden,
das sind: sechsundachtzig Millionen und vierhunderttausend hundertstel oder achthundertvier-
undsechzigtausend ganze Sekunden oder vierzehntausendvierhundert Minuten, zweihundert-
vierzig Stunden oder ganze zehn Tage … tatsächlich begann am 22. Dezember schon das
neue Jahr … von dem an die Tage wieder länger, und die Nächte kürzer werden; Winterson-
nenwende … doch der Teufel steckt im Detail und hat doch ein gewisser Silvester alles über
den Haufen geschmissen, konnte angeblich das Neue Jahr am 23. nicht begrüßen weil er sich
unglücklicherweise gerade mal naßgemacht hatte, zehn Tage trocknen mußte und erst am 1.
Januar soweit war, daß er das, inzwischen schon recht alte, Neue Jahr endlich begrüßen konnte … da er aber sein Mißgeschick vertuschen wollte, und eben einer dieser Leithammel war,
befahl er dem 1. Januar; Neujahr und Silvester in eins zu sein …

the Teutons, Celts, Britons, all of them knew the beginning of the new year … the
"enlightened" lustful new age funsociety doesn´t know it … has littered its consciousness
with having fun, being free and believing in progress … about one hundred years ago, Thor
Heyerdahl came to the conclusion: progress means, in the end, regress from Paradise … at
any rate will the civilized brainless mankind herd not be able to realize that … and will
probably mess on like that … on, to the bitter end … happy New Year! …

die alten Germanen, Kelten, Briten, alle wußten wann das neue Jahr beginnt … die „aufge-
klärte" geile new age Fungesellschaft weiß das nicht … hat ihr Bewußtsein mit Spaß haben,
frei sein und Fortschrittsglaube vollgemüllt … um die Jahrhundertwende, vor rund hundert
Jahren schon, hat Thor Heyerdahl diagnostiziert: Fortschritt ist Fortschritt vom Paradies …
natürlich bergeift das die durch eben diesen „Fortschritt" gehirnamputierte Menschenherde
nicht … und wird wohl bis zum bitteren Ende so weitermachen …
frohes Neues Jahr! …

12.30 p.m.
high time to open the window for my big friend … so he might fly back towards his home-
area and arrive there before nightfall – hoping, no human will be up to mischief there …

12.30 Uhr
nun wird es höchste Zeit meinem großen Vogel das Fenster zu öffnen … daß er bis zum
Abend dorthin wo er zu Hause ist zurückgefunden hat wo, hoffentlich, weit und breit kein
Mensch sein Unwesen treibt …

the window hasn´t been closed for long when my next winged guest arrives – badly rumpled
by a fight with a crow, and the box, from which he emerges like the spirit from the bottle –

das Fenster war noch nicht allzulange geschlossen als mein nächster
gefiederter Gast ankommt -
zerzaust vom Kampf mit einer Krähe, und dem Karton, kommt er aus ihm heraus wie der
Geist aus der Flasche –

Karl just brought him to me, hidden in the cartoon he was said to be a buzzard, in
the meantime he became a ??? – he must be very hungry, because the crow didn't want
him to eat her, and more – if such a small bird tries to eat such a big and powerful bird as
crows are, he must, at that time, have already been driven mad by starvation …
I offer him a piece of beef –

Karl hat ihn mir eben gebracht, verborgen im Karton war er angeblich noch ein Bussard,
inzwischen ist aus ihm ein ??? geworden – er muß sehr hungrig sein, denn die
Krähe hat sich ja nicht von ihm verspeisen lassen, und wenn ein so kleiner Kerl es mit einer
so viel größeren, dazu recht wehrhaften Krähe versucht, muß ihn der Hunger schon in den
Wahnsinn getrieben haben … biete ihm erstmal ein Stückchen Rindfleisch an –

asks what shall I do with this – flies on Karl´s head, who has just taken this photo, and on to the table – pause – if our new guest had known how tasty this piece of beef actually is, he ´d have torn it from my hand, starved as he is, having no respect for me nor any sign of fear, like someone that is very familiar with humans, having experienced their community – nevertheless is it very unlikely that he might have been looked after by humans since he isn´t acquainted with beef … and now I ´d like to have him taste …

fragt sich; was soll ich da denn mit - fliegt Karl, der dieses Photo von uns gerade gemacht hat, auf den Kopf und weiter auf den Tisch – Pause – wüßte unser neuer Gast wie lecker ihm Rindfleisch schmecken wird, würde er es, ausgehungert wie er ist, mir nur so aus den Fingern reißen, denn Respekt oder gar Angst scheint er vor mir ja nun überhaupt nicht zu haben, wie jemand dem Menschen vertraut sind, der mit Menschen schon mal zusammengelebt hat – daß diesem Vogel Rindfleisch aber fremd ist läßt vermuten, daß er noch nie von Menschen betreut worden ist … und wie Rindfleisch schmeckt möchte ich ihm nun zeigen …

rather dubious he looks at me as my hand offers him a piece of beef, and, when I hold his beak between my thumb and forefinger and rub the beef gently across the closed beak … it opens a little – a wee tip of a tongue emerges and plays …

befremdet sieht er auf mich herab, wie sich meine Hand mit einem Stückchen Fleisch seinem Gesicht nähert, hält gebannt still als ich seinen Schnabel zwischen Daumen und Zeigefinger nehme und das Fleisch seitlich über den geschlossenen Spalt streiche … der Spalt öffnet sich ein wenig, eine kleine Zungenspitze züngelt hervor und …

wild sparrow-hawks are extremely shy – experts have told me – they won´t take any food
while humans are in sight – when I told them about the behavior of this sparrow-hawk they
wouldn´t believe it … my friend and I, we believe, in each other …

wilde Sperber sind so scheu – haben Experten mir versichert – daß sie in Gegenwart von
Menschen die Nahrung verweigern – als sie erfahren wie dieser Sperber sich bei mir verhält,
verstehen sie die Welt nicht mehr … wir aber, mein Freund und ich, wir verstehen …

let me have it …   gib schon …

sunbath on the printer …   Sonnenbad auf dem Drucker …

happy to be friends …   glücklich in unserer Freundschaft …

he watches me while I´m writing our story …

schaut mir zu wie ich unsere Geschichte schreibe …

enjoys his meal on top of the screen … läßt sich sein Mahl auf dem Bildschirm schmecken …

on the computer …   auf dem computer …

anywhere …   überall …

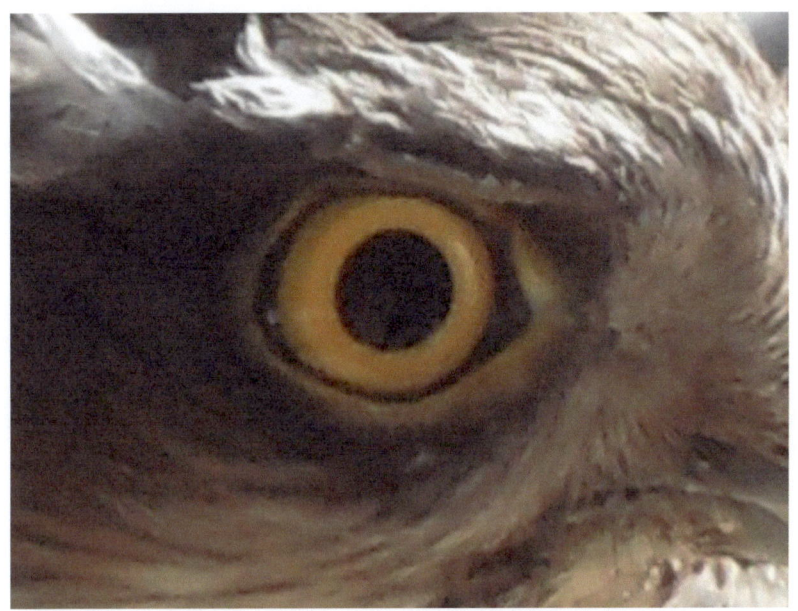

deep in there you´ll find the birds soul …tief da drinnen kannst du die Vogelseele finden ...

loves water …   liebt Wasser …

after bathing, grooming …   nach dem Bad, Gefiederpflege …

dreamflight in his secret world .,.   Traumflug in seine geheime Welt …

the birds would stay round about three birdmoons, I guessed, when the first child-birds
arrived – but, which birdmoon may this one be now? …

drei Vogelmonde lang könnten die Vögel wohl bei mir sein, hab ich so gedacht, als die ersten Vogelkinder zu mir kamen – und nun?, der wievielte Mond wird dieser wohl sein? …

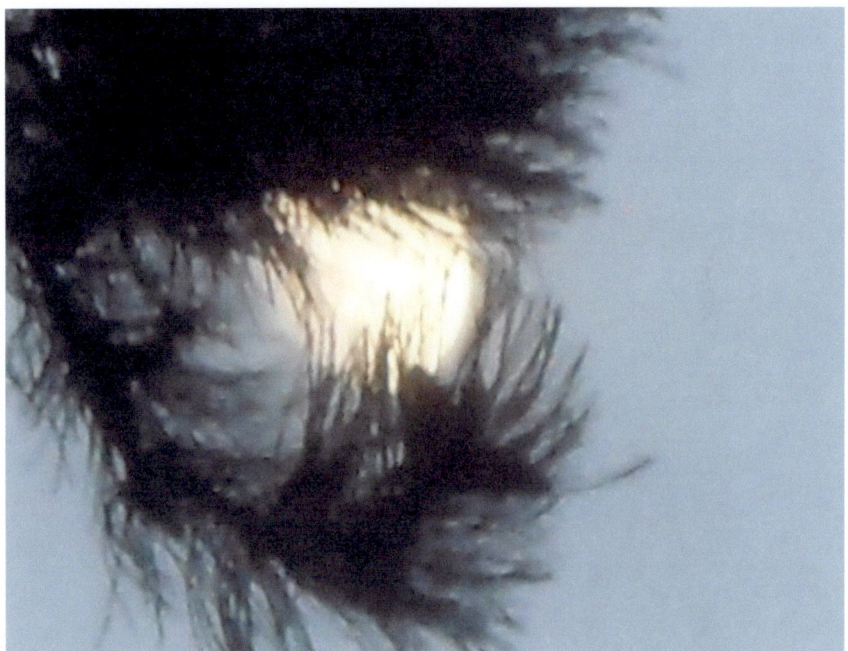

what destiny may now be hidden in this new day? Monday, 13th of June 2011? …

und was wird der neue Tag wohl mit sich bringen? Montag der 13. Juni 2011? …

early in the morning it will begin, the adventure with the baby-blackbirds ...
Nadin and I have narrated about it already some time ago in the "Three Bird-moons" ...
it is our first bird-story published as an ebook on the internet – three bird-moons originally
meant those tales, that wander, like an endless chain, through time and space ...
when orphand bird-babies arrived in summer 2010, I began to write their story,
expecting all birds would leave the scene within three months, so "Three Bird-moons"
would suit their tale – "Three Bird-years" would be better by now – well, it is as it is;
the title: "Three Bird-moons" got stuck to the first ebook, so all other tales will
be named: xxxxxxxxx from Three Bird-moons ...

am frühen Morgen wird es beginnen, das Abenteuer mit den Amselbabys ...
davon haben Nadine und ich aber schon längst erzählt, in den „Drei Vogelmonde" ...
das ist unsere erste Vogelgeschichte die als ebook im internet erscheint – mit drei

Vogelmonden waren ursprünglich Erzählungen gemeint, die, in endloser Kette, durch Raum und Zeit wandern ... als, wie schon so oft, mal wieder elternlose Vögel zu uns kamen, das war noch im Sommer 2010, und ich zu schreiben begann, glaubte ich, daß die Geschichte höchstens drei Monde währen würde, und „Drei Vogelmonde" heißen könnte – „Drei Vogeljahre" würde inzwischen eher hinkommen – nun ist „Drei Vogelmonde" an dem ersten ebook hängengelieben, worauf all die anderen Geschichten: xxxxxxxxx aus Drei Vogelmonde heißen werden ...

ever so many bird-tales occured – birds come and go like days come and go – dream comes, and nightmare comes, and happy dreams and it is, altogether, just one eternal experience narrated by one never ending sentence, actually, and that´s why I use one capital letter only at the beginning of this long, long sentence and no fullstop and capital letters chopping it all to pieces – that´s my humble contribution to a new style of writing ...

sooo viele Vogelgeschichten habe ich erlebt – Vögel kommen und gehen wie die Tage kommen und gehen – Traum und Albtraum und wieder Traum, auch manch glücklicher Traum, und es ist ein unendliches Erleben in einen endlosen Satz gebettet erzählt, und deshalb schreibe ich auch nur das erste Wort des langen, langen Satzes der Geschichte groß – daß nicht Punkte und große Buchstaben Satz und Geschichte zerhacken können – mein bescheidener Beitrag zu einer mal sinnvollen Rechtschreibreform ...

birds come and go like days come and go – dream comes, and nightmare comes, and happy dreams are coming too, and now there comes a luckless bird, and with it a nightmare is coming in ... the joint of its right leg is broken, its shank dangling with every movement – and hurts badly and can´t be mended and is so very afraid of its fate – doomed to starve to death, if no miracle happens ...

Vögel kommen und gehen wie Tage kommen und gehen – Träume kommen, und Albträume kommen, und glückliche Träume kommen auch, und jetzt erscheint hier ein glückloser Vogel mit einem Albtraum im Gepäck ... sein rechtes Bein ist im Gelenk gebrochen, schlenkert bei jeder Bewegung hin und her und schmerzt und kann nicht geheilt werden, und fürchtet sich vor seinem Schicksal – zum Hungertod verdammt, wenn kein Wunder geschieht ...

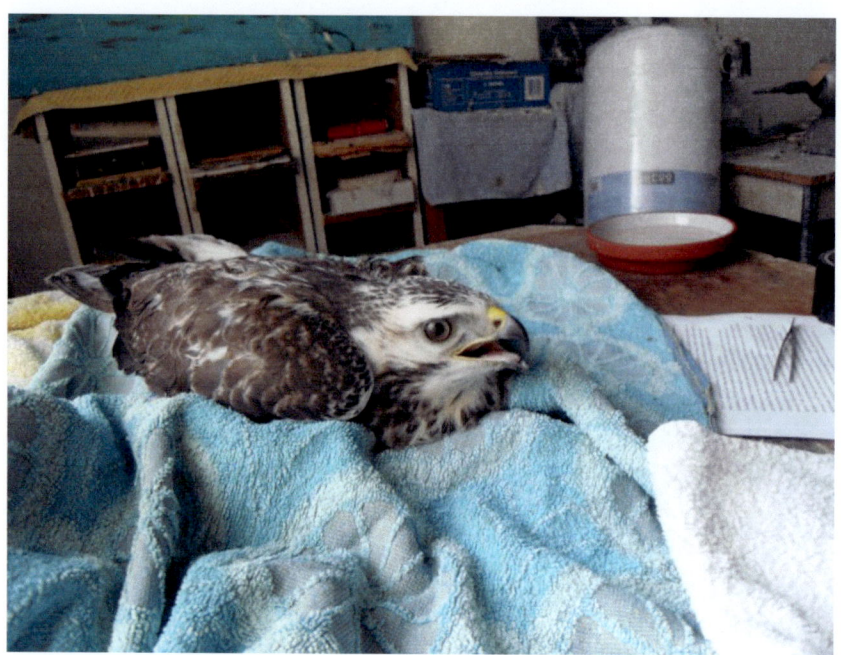

paralised by fright, doesn´t dare to move …   angsterstarrt liegt er da und rührt sich nicht …

a farmer has brought him to my care, and wonders why the bird keeps his beak open all the
time – well, probably the man has tomatoes on his eyes and turnips in his soul, so he can't
see that utmost distress in this birds eyes – but his heart is in the right spot, and for that I
can´t help but love him … that´s how it is – blindfold, ignorant, but a big heart!,
whished there were more farmers like him … I simply dare not imagine what usually is going
on many farms all over the world …

ein Bauer hat ihn mir in meine Obhut gegeben, und kann sich nicht erklären warum der Vogel
die ganze Zeit seinen Schnabel aufhält – ja, der Mann hat wohl Tomaten auf den Augen, und
Steckrüben auf der Seele, daß er die verzweifelte Angst in den Augen dieses Vogels nicht
sehen kann – sein Herz aber ist am rechten Fleck – drum muß ich ihn auch einfach lieb haben
… ja, so geht das – gesegnet mit Unwissenheit, aber ein großes Herz! wenn es nur viele
solche Bauern gäbe! … ich mag nicht daran denken wie so viele Bauern mit den ihnen
auf Gedeih und Verderb ausgelieferten Tieren umgehen … weltweit …

Nadine appears, and with her the miracle ...   Nadine erscheint, und mit ihr das Wunder ...

in stead of looking at a photo, just imagine
the healing hands of a women who will of
course present her hands to an injured bird,
but not to the public – she insists on canceling
her image here ...

an dieser Stelle muß man sich die heilenden
Hände einer Frau vorstellen, die ihre Hände
wohl dem verletzten Vogel, nicht aber der
Allgemeinheit schenken möchte, und nicht
will, daß sie hier abgebildet sind ...

Nadines hands and her loving care, will try to do the miracle
that shall heal this birds broken joint …

Nadines Hände, und ihre liebende Fürsorge werden versuchen das Wunder zu bewirken das
das gebrochene Gelenk dieses Vogels heilen wird …

quite at rest have Nadines fingers investigated this buzzard´s leg and pondered, till they were
sure to know whether they should make the bandage tight or loose as would be best …

lange, mit großer Ruhe haben Nadines Finger des Bussards Bein erforscht und nachgedacht,
bis sie wußten wie sie den Verband, wie locker und wie fest, anlegen sollten …

poor soul, so utterly afraid …   arme Seele, die nackte Angst im Gesicht …

after the torture, he hides away …   nach der Folter, schnell verstecken …

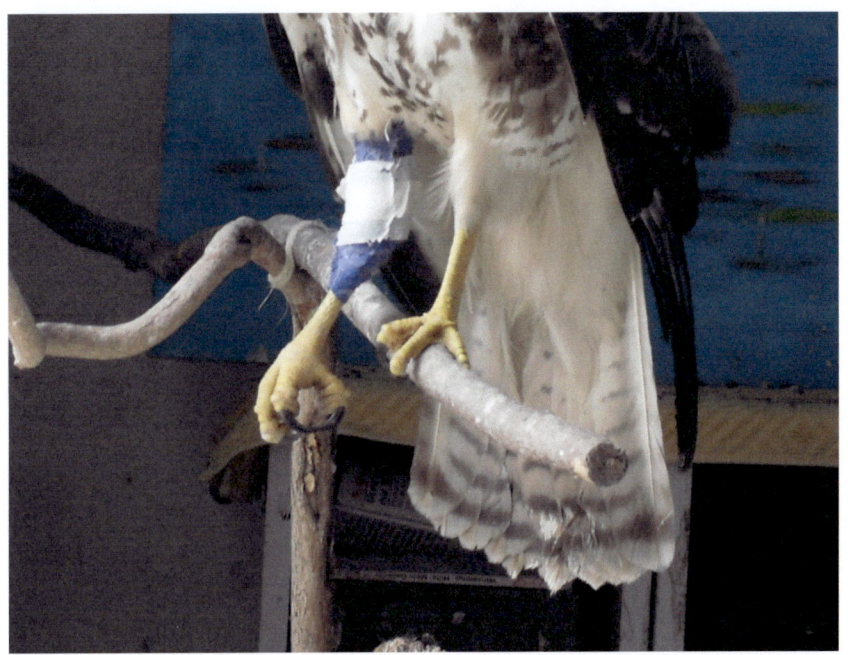

it doesn't look good …   das sieht nicht gut aus …

trying to land on both feet …   versucht auf beiden Füßen zu landen …

landed, his grip half open …   gelandet, den Griff halb geöffnet …

it doesn't look too bad now any more – two weeks have passed since this beautiful bird was given into my care, and this time no friendship arose … but, as we shall get to know looking at the next page: Nadine indeed has performed a miracle …

nun sieht es gar nicht mehr so schlecht aus – zwei Wochen sind vergangen seit dieser wunderschöne Vogel mir anvertraut wurde – eine Freundschaft ist zwischen uns nicht entstanden … aber, die nächste Seite wird es uns zeigen:

Nadine hat ein Wunder vollbracht …

on his favourite perch …   auf seinem Lieblingsplatz …

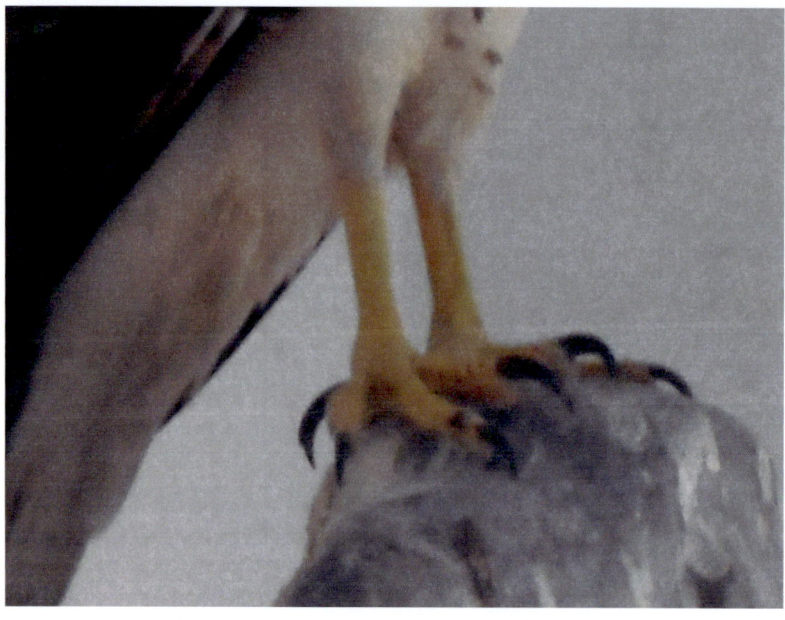

the miracle …   das Wunder …

now I will open the window for him …   nun werde ich ihm das Fenster öffnen …